**HENRY**

**JAMES**

**PERCY**

# TITLES AVAILABLE IN BUZZ BOOKS

First published 1990 by Buzz Books,
an imprint of the Octopus Publishing Group,
Michelin House, 81 Fulham Road, London SW3 6RB

LONDON  MELBOURNE  AUCKLAND

Copyright © William Heinemann Ltd 1990

All publishing rights: William Heinemann Ltd. All television
and merchandising rights licensed by William Heinemann Ltd
to Britt Allcroft (Thomas) Ltd exclusively, worldwide.

Photographs © Britt Allcroft (Thomas) Ltd 1985
Photographs by David Mitton and Kenny McArthur
for Britt Allcroft's production of
Thomas the Tank Engine and Friends.

ISBN 1 85591 028 4

Printed and bound in the UK by BPCC Paulton Books Ltd.

# THOMAS AND THE TRUCKS

**buzz books**

Thomas the Tank Engine wouldn't stop being a nuisance. Night after night he kept the other engines awake.

"I'm tired of pushing coaches. I want to see the world."

The other engines didn't take much notice, for Thomas was a little engine with a long tongue.

But one night, Edward came to the shed.

He was a kind little engine, and felt sorry for Thomas.

"I've got some trucks to take home tomorrow."

"If you take them instead of me I'll push coaches in the yard."

"Thank you," said Thomas, "that will be nice."

Next morning Edward and Thomas asked their drivers, and when they said "Yes," Thomas ran off happily to find the trucks.

Now trucks are silly and noisy. They talk a lot and don't attend to what they are doing.

And I'm sorry to say, they play tricks on an engine who is not used to them.

Edward knew all about trucks. He warned Thomas to be careful, but Thomas was too excited to listen.

The shunter fastened the coupling, and when the signal dropped Thomas was ready.

The guard blew his whistle.

"Peep! Peep!" answered Thomas and started off.

But the trucks weren't ready.

"Oh, oh, oh," they screamed. "Wait Thomas, wait."

But Thomas wouldn't wait.

"Come on, come on," he puffed.

"All right, all right, don't fuss, all right, don't fuss," grumbled the trucks.

Thomas began going faster and faster.

"Wheeeee," he whistled, as he rushed through Henry's tunnel.

Then he was out into the open countryside once more.

They rumbled past fields and they clattered through stations.

"Hurry, hurry," called Thomas.

He was feeling very proud of himself.

But the trucks grew crosser and crosser.

At last Thomas slowed down as he came to Gordon's hill.

"Steady now, steady," warned the driver, as they reached the top.

He began to put on the brakes.

"We're stopping, we're stopping," called Thomas.

"No, no, no, no!" answered the trucks, bumping into each other.

"Go on, go on."

Before the driver could stop them, they had pushed Thomas down the hill and were rattling and laughing behind him.

Poor Thomas tried hard to stop them from making him go too fast.

"Stop pushing, stop pushing," he hissed, but the trucks took no notice.

"Go on, go on," they giggled in their silly way.

Thomas was travelling much too fast and at any moment he would reach the next station.

20

"There's the station. Oh dear, what shall I do?" he cried.

They rattled straight through and swerved into the goods yard.

Thomas shut his eyes. "I must stop."

When he opened his eyes he saw he had stopped just in front of the buffers.

There watching him was the
Fat Controller.

"What are you doing here, Thomas?" he asked.

"I've brought Edward's trucks," Thomas answered.

"Why did you come so fast?"

"I didn't mean to. I was pushed," said Thomas.